JEANETTE WINTER

Cowboy Charlie

THE STORY OF CHARLES M. RUSSELL

Harcourt Brace & Company

SAN DIEGO   NEW YORK   LONDON

Requests for permission to make copies of any part of the work should be mailed to:
Permissions Department, Harcourt Brace & Company,
6277 Sea Harbor Drive, Orlando, Florida 32887–6777.

Library of Congress Cataloging-in-Publication Data
Winter, Jeanette
Cowboy Charlie:the story of Charles M. Russell/Jeanette Winter.—1st ed.
p. cm.
ISBN 0-15-200857-8
1. Russell, Charles M. (Charles Marion), 1864-1926—Juvenile literature.
2. Painters—United States—Biography—Juvenile literature.
3. West (U.S.) in art—Juvenile literature.
[1. Russell, Charles M. (Charles Marion), 1864-1926.
2. Artists. 3. West (U.S.) in art.] I. Title.
ND237.R75W56   1995
759.13—dc20   94-48480

Printed in Singapore
First edition A B C D E

The illustrations in this book were done in acrylics on Strathmore Bristol.
The display type was set in Giddyup by the Photocomposition Center,
Harcourt Brace & Company, San Diego, California.
The text type was set in Holland Seminar by the Photocompostion Center,
Harcourt Brace & Company, San Diego, California.
Color separations by Bright Arts, Ltd., Singapore
Printed and bound by Tien Wah Press, Singapore
This book was printed with soya-based inks on Leykam recycled paper,
which contains more than 20 percent postconsumer waste and has
a total recycled content of at least 50 percent.
Production supervision by Warren Wallerstein and Ginger Boyer
Designed by Jeanette Winter, Gunta Alexander, and Lori J. McThomas

To the Winter brothers,
Jonah and Max

In the days when buffalo still roamed in the West,
Charles Marion Russell was born in the city of St. Louis,
far, far away from those Western plains. He had four brothers
and one sister and a pony named Jip and a dog named Tige
and a mother and a father who all loved him.

On rainy days, Charlie's father read stories about Davy Crockett and
Daniel Boone and Kit Carson, and told tales of his great-uncle Bent,
a fur trader in the Old West.

Charlie listened closely and drew pictures of his heroes.

On sunny days in summer, the woods behind Grandpa's house became the Wild West.

Charlie roped make-believe cows as he and Jip rode across the gully to Uncle George's house.

On snowy days in winter, Charlie made his own Western world, fashioned out of beeswax scraps from sister Sue's wax flowers.

On dark nights when he couldn't sleep, Charlie looked up at the sky and dreamed of sleeping under a roof of stars, like the cowboys did.

While the teacher at school talked about arithmetic, Charlie's thoughts were far away.

As he grew older, he often played hooky from school. Charlie could be found down at the riverfront of the Mississippi, listening to the fur traders and mountain men tell tall tales of the West.

He dreamed of joining them.

When Charlie was fifteen years old, and still dreaming of the West, his mother and father let him go to Montana Territory with "Pike" Miller, a sheep rancher and family friend. They thought a month in the wilderness would chase his Western dreams away.

Charlie and Pike rode the train to Red Rock, where the tracks ended. They loaded their bags onto a stagecoach and continued on into the wilderness.

Holding a buffalo skull he found while the horses rested, Charlie saw the country of his dreams unfold before him.

They pulled into Last Chance Gulch, the wild and woolly town of Helena. The stagecoach went no farther. Charlie's eyes opened wide when he saw all the mule skinners, miners, mountain men, Indians, bull teams, and freight outfits that lined the streets. Charlie was at the frontier.

But the ranch was still a long way off. Pike outfitted them with two saddle horses, two packhorses, and supplies for the final leg of their journey. Charlie outfitted himself as a cowboy, adding his own touch— a bright French-Indian sash.

Charlie and Pike rode out across the plains. And then, one month after leaving St. Louis, they finally reached the country of Pike's ranch in the Judith Basin. Spring had arrived with the two weary travelers.

As Charlie listened to the red-winged blackbird sing its song to the antelope, he knew he would never leave this paradise.

Charlie's first job was herding sheep for Pike. But he lost the sheep as fast as they were put on the ranch. He lost his job, too.

Charlie headed off alone for the Judith River, with his few belongings and his horse, Monte. He camped by the river, wondering what to do next.

As Charlie sat modeling his tiny beeswax animals, a bearded stranger rode up.

He introduced himself as Jake Hoover.

Jake was a kindhearted hunter and trapper who lived in nearby Pig-eye Basin. He took Charlie under his wing and invited him to share his small cabin.

Charlie was grateful and went to live with Jake, and at night listened to the stories Jake told.

During the day, Charlie was Jake's helper as he hunted in the mountains. He learned all about the bears and beaver and elk and mountain sheep and deer who lived there.

But Charlie still wanted to be a cowboy.

After two winters with Jake, Charlie finally landed a job in the spring roundup as a nighthawk. He guarded the cowboys' horses, all four hundred of them, all night long. Even on stormy nights, Charlie loved his new life. At last he was a cowboy.

The men traded tales around the campfire. Charlie remembered their stories to paint later. And sometimes "Kid" Russell, as the older cowboys called eighteen-year-old Charlie, was the storyteller. With the twinkle that was always in his eye, he spun yarns that made the cowhands smile.

At dawn, Charlie would come in from herding and sleep for a few hours. Then he painted and sketched everything he saw around the cow camp—bronco riding, branding, and roping.

And he painted on anything he could find—cracker boxes, birch bark, backs of envelopes, mirrors, or buckskin.

After a summer of herding cattle and branding calves, the cowboys began the long drive to market. For two months, the cowhands kept the herd moving, through Judith Gap, down Swimming Woman Creek, on to the Yellowstone River, to Pompey's Pillar, to Froze to Death Creek, over a divide to Sunday Creek, and on to the end of the trail at Miles City.

The cowboys showed Charlie where Indian battles had taken place along the trail. And he saw riders from different tribes. Charlie's paints and brushes were always with him, stowed away in a sock that hung on his saddle horn. While the herd rested, he painted what he had seen.

When the work was done one fall, Charlie went north and lived with the Blood Indians. Charlie's friend Sleeping Thunder gave him the Indian name for antelope—Ah-Wah-Cous.

Charlie sketched and painted all winter, and his Blood friends loved his pictures as much as his cowboy friends did.

Ah-Wah-Cous learned the Blood language and sat with his friends around the fire at night, remembering their stories and legends to paint later.

After the snow melted, Charlie returned for the spring roundup. By now he was a night herder, singing to hundreds and hundreds of cattle in the moonlight. Charlie looked up at the stars. He was glad to be a cowboy.

Charlie sang to the cattle for many years.
But the West was changing.
The railroad cut through the plains,
bringing settlers, towns, and locked doors.
Barbed-wire fences were everywhere.
The great herds of buffalo were gone.
Charlie did not like the changes.

He stopped singing to the horses and cattle,
and settled into a log cabin studio,
and painted the stories he had heard
from the cowpunchers and mountain men,
and the tales and legends of the Indians,
and all his years as a cowboy,
and told the story of the Wild West.

About Charles Marion Russell

After giving up his work as a cowboy in 1892, Charles Russell became a full-time artist. His paintings and sculptures can be seen at the C. M. Russell Museum in Great Falls, Montana, and in art museums across the country.

A statue of Charles Russell, representing the state of Montana, stands in the Rotunda of the U.S. Capitol in Washington, D.C. Russell is the only artist so honored in the Capitol's Statuary Hall.

Russell died in 1926, after opening the door to the West to so many.